KAYLA'S GIFT

JAYNE RYLON

eBook ISBN: 978-1-941785-30-0
Print ISBN: 978-1-941785-58-4

Ebook Cover Art By Angela Waters
Print Book Cover Art By Jayne Rylon
Interior Print Book Design By Jayne Rylon

OTHER BOOKS BY JAYNE RYLON

DIVEMASTERS
Going Down
Going Deep
Going Hard

MEN IN BLUE
Night is Darkest
Razor's Edge
Mistress's Master
Spread Your Wings
Wounded Hearts
Bound For You

POWERTOOLS
Kate's Crew
Morgan's Surprise
Kayla's Gift
Devon's Pair
Nailed to the Wall
Hammer it Home

HOTRODS

King Cobra
Mustang Sally
Super Nova
Rebel on the Run
Swinger Style
Barracuda's Heart
Touch of Amber
Long Time Coming

COMPASS BROTHERS

Northern Exposure
Southern Comfort
Eastern Ambitions
Western Ties

COMPASS GIRLS

Winter's Thaw
Hope Springs
Summer Fling
Falling Softly

PLAY DOCTOR

Dream Machine
Healing Touch

DEDICATION

To Angela Waters, cover artist extraordinaire, for bringing the crew to life in all of the fabulous Powertools covers (twice now).

Thank you!

CHAPTER ONE

"Oh God, that's good."

"Harder?" Kayla intensified her motion when the man beneath her groaned.

"Yeah. Right there. Don't stop, baby."

"No worries, I'll take care of you."

"Always do." Dave sighed. "I look forward to coming inside all damn day. It's tough to concentrate when your gifted hands are waiting for me."

"But if you weren't aggravating this strained muscle by building my spa, you wouldn't need my fabulous massages."

"Is it any wonder I love my job?"

Kayla's fingers drifted from Dave's sculpted shoulders to tug the silky hair feathering over the nape of his neck. As if she minded his near-constant teasing.

Her work rocked pretty solid too—at least when it involved touching prime specimens of masculinity like Dave. While she lingered, she rubbed along his spine, eliciting another deep purr. The rumble curled her bare toes in the plush area rug.

"And here I thought the highlight of your career was your kick-ass partners." A gruff rebuke from the general direction of the entrance startled Kayla.

Dave's gorgeous body had consumed her focus. Bold ridges of sinew tempted her fingers to explore beyond the requirements of his treatment. She'd never seen anatomy so fine outside of her textbooks. Lying on his toned abdomen, the bull of a man threatened to destroy her portable table with his defined bulk.

She couldn't wait for the permanent equipment she'd ordered to arrive.

Furnishing her new facility would be the final step in bringing her vision to life.

"You guys aren't bad, either." Dave angled his head to face Mike, the construction crew's foreman, who leaned his hip on the doorjamb. Her patient didn't scramble for a towel to cover his smoking-hot ass or flinch in the slightest. The muscles she'd worked so hard to relax stayed pliant. "What's up, boss?"

"There's a hell of a storm brewing outside. The snow's started, and the sky is black as shit. Joe and I are heading back to town. Our girls are worried. Kate's called twice. Morgan texted enough times to overflow the screen of Joe's phone. Neither one of them are naggers by nature. The unpaved section of the road turns into a skating rink when all those puddles freeze over. Too much longer and we'll all be stuck."

"They're forecasting what, a foot and a half, now?"

Kayla attacked the tension invading Dave.

"Nah, they upped the projection again. More like two to three." Mike shook his head. "Plus, the wind is kicking in. Froze my balls off on the roof, but we finished shingling in time."

She raised an eyebrow in his direction without faltering in her caresses.

"Crap, sorry. Anyway, James and Neil are making one last round, lashing tarps over our supplies and Kayla's firewood while you pamper that knot in your shoulder. Pussy."

"Yeah, yeah." Dave's broad back flexed beneath her fingers. "Jealous?"

"Hardly. No offense, Kayla."

"None taken."

"My Kate is the only woman who can heal me with her touch."

Kayla sighed. "Someday I'll meet a man who adores *me*, right?"

"Hell-ooo. Last time I checked, I was a dude." Dave squinted at her. "Didn't I tell you how much I love you less than two minutes ago?"

He had. Damn if the lame joke hadn't wreaked havoc on her hormones too. She knew better than to imagine his constant flirtations were more than habit. The guys in the crew had "player" stamped all over their hard bodies in between their bold tattoos. She traced an organic swirl of red ink around Dave's shoulder.

"Okay, kids. Before you become bicker buddies again, I'm heading out." Mike's grin slipped a fraction of an inch. "Are you sure you have everything you need, Kayla? It could be a while before we can make it back. I don't like the thought of you up here. Alone. My offer stands. Stay with Kate and me. You'd be friends inside a minute, I bet. The two of you could stir up a world of trouble together. Throw Morgan in the mix and..."

"God help us." Dave grunted when she pressed her elbow into the base of his spine.

"Thanks, but no thanks. Kate and Morgan sound like a riot though." Their respective fiancé and boyfriend talked about the women pretty near constantly.

"Come home with us and hang out." Dave tried again. "It'll be fun, not to mention safe."

"No different than here. James and Neil brought a mountain of groceries this morning. You checked the generator at least a thousand times." Kayla's lips curved as she contemplated the high potential for peaceful solitude. Her and a world blanketed in white. An occasional deer for company. "Really. I'm fine. Thank you."

"All righty then." Mike crossed to her and dropped a kiss on the top of her head.

She took advantage of the distraction to adjust her sweater away from her beading nipples, hoping the men couldn't detect the small hoops in them. An irregular beat of her heart fluttered her chest.

When any member of the crew stood so near, denying their potent charm became impossible. Wedged between two of the studs, she could hardly breathe. Every one of the guys rocketed straight off her hotness chart, each with his unique twist. Mike's fraternal care warmed her despite the chill creeping through the giant plate-glass window, which overlooked the mountainside and the lake in the distance. The flash of heat he inspired, though brilliant, was like a match compared to the bonfire Dave's searing sexuality lit inside her.

"Stay safe. I'm gone. Dave, you and the dynamic duo better hit the road as soon as they're finished." Mike slapped her patient on the ass and called over his retreating shoulder, "Five minutes or less. Start packing this away."

Kayla wondered at the easy confidence the crew possessed around each other.

"Hey, can I ask you something?" She grimaced when the thought flew off her lips. Great, now she'd introduce awkwardness to their light friendship.

"Anything."

She continued to work on Dave, gathering her courage while she kneaded the flushed red handprint Mike had left on Dave's right cheek. Her fingers trailed to the backs of his powerful thighs before she continued. "Most of my clients freak at the idea of someone spying their naughty bits, especially if my treatment... arouses them."

Neither she nor Dave could deny the solid erection he sported every time she touched him. Hiding his impressive equipment would have been near impossible even if he'd bothered to try. The guys who'd helped her bring her dream to life—by constructing a quaint log cabin to house her future lakeside retreat—never once hesitated to drop trou or practiced the floor-tile-meet-laser-beam-stare, which she'd witnessed from others, when she offered to rub them down in the presence of their crewmates.

"So?"

"You guys don't worry about stuff like that. If things get too intimate for one of you, you simply roll over, gather your clothes and put your—"

"Cock."

"Yeah." They'd tuck their junk into their ripped, paint-stained jeans. She shivered. "You zip up with no apologies. No false denials. No shame. More like a polite kiss on the cheek and a thank you."

"Why should we be ashamed? You're sexy as sin and fan-fucking-tastic with your hands." He grinned up at her. "Does it bother you to know you turn us on?"

"Hell no! When people act like a natural reaction is some giant secret, they sometimes make me feel like I've done something dirty." The crew's lack of inhibitions refreshed her, gave her hope her crazy venture could work. "Your honesty is nice. Uncommon."

"You could say a lot of our relationship is unique. Me and the rest of the guys in the crew are close. We don't hide stuff from each other. We share everything without assuming attraction has to lead to action. I'm not gonna lie, though. It's great when it does."

If she hadn't been so lost in thought, she might have probed for more info.

They had no idea she planned more than an ordinary sanctuary surrounded by the wilderness outside. Not yet, anyway. She'd considered sharing her dream once she discovered how open-minded they were, but the opportunity hadn't arisen during the lunch breaks she shared with them or the massage sessions she supplied to discount her bill. They were usually too busy—pulling pranks, telling her wild stories or raising hell—to sit and chat.

She loved every minute of their company. Still, she'd fork over her autographed copy of Walt Whitman's *A Sun-Bath—Nakedness*, or at least grant a peek at the rare document, for a sounding board.

Kayla intended to open a nudist getaway. A spa where people could roam free of clothes and recriminating glares. Naked was her style. After her impulsive purchase of the acreage surrounding them, she'd spent loads of time on the mountain by herself. She'd indulged in both the luxury and the wildness of shucking her trappings plenty before hiring the five sexy men who comprised the crew to bring her vision to reality.

Her family and friends had called the venture everything from ridiculous to a poor manifestation of her free spirit. The team of professionals—two lawyers, a doctor and an accountant—her parents had bred couldn't comprehend the whims of their odd little sister.

"Hey, you okay?"

She blinked. When had Dave moved? He dragged faded denim over his lean hips. Damn it. She licked her lips as he tugged on a thin gray T-shirt, which obscured his firm pecs, then his six-pack and finally the ridge caused by his inguinal ligament—her absolute favorite spot on a man's body. She could lick the crest it created from his hip straight to his…

"Kayla?" Dave rested his broad hand on her elbow, shaking her from the daydream.

Shit! For a woman considering founding a naturist haven, she certainly had a hard time separating this man's form from his radiant attractiveness. A problem she'd never had before.

"Change your mind about staying? You can bunk with me if you're not interested in plugging your ears to block out the soundtrack accompanying all the sex rocking Mike and Kate's apartment."

She laughed. "Nah, I'm good. Ready for a couple quiet days, that's all."

"You're not sleeping enough."

No kidding. If she didn't order supplies, build a website, draft design concepts and secure the funding remaining to fill the gap after her sibling's generous contributions, who would?

"Yes, Dad."

"Fuck. Sorry. It's none of my business—"

"If her *friends* can't tell it like it is, who can?" Another heckler waltzed in on their conversation.

"James." She hugged Dave in a quick, silent apology as the slighter man neared. "You're right. Both of you. I promise to take a little time off to enjoy the season. You know, frolic in the snow and crap."

"Damn straight you will." Neil joined them in the suddenly cramped area. How had it seemed spacious to her before? "Not much else you'll be able to accomplish anyway. It's turning nasty."

Kayla ushered them out of her living room and onto the front porch, crossing her arms over her chest to ward off the intense chill. It could be a hundred below yet she'd rather endure the sting of the wind for a couple seconds than add another layer of clothing to her frame.

The more she went nude, the more it stifled her to be dressed. The holidays she'd spent with her family had driven her insane with discomfort. A few moments longer and she could retreat to the bliss of her fireplace.

Dave tugged on his leather jacket while the other two men piled into their beast of a truck.

"Drive safe."

Now that the guys prepared to pull out of her yard, a rebellious fraction of her mind wished she'd accepted Dave's offer. Several days without their easy company seemed like an awfully long time. How could that be when she'd only met them six weeks earlier?

"We will." He buttoned the flattering coat, inspiring a gulp.

She'd never seen him wear the thing before, never mind fasten it to the neck. Sporting something so constricting would suffocate her. Still, she wouldn't complain about the extra time his actions granted them.

"Call if you need anything, baby."

Like a hot construction worker to keep me toasty? Hopping from foot to foot to prevent her toes from numbing—still preferable than stuffing them into the prison of heavy shoes—she indulged her stubborn streak, which refused to abandon the porch until he'd vanished from sight. She chaffed her arms. Snowflakes swirled around them, drifting onto her hair. When one landed on her bottom lip, she licked the miniature puddle it left behind.

Dave's eyes slitted a moment before he growled, "Fuck this."

Kayla gasped between his parted lips when he swooped in to taste the moisture for himself. The kiss caught her completely off guard. He hadn't telegraphed a single hint he'd noticed the electricity arcing between them. Not once had he taken their flirtation beyond harmless.

Until now.

She sank into his loose hold.

His tongue stole its first taste of her mouth. The gust of passion he inspired knocked her off balance. She wrapped her arms around his neck to keep from losing her footing. When she thought she might try to crawl up him right there at the top of her stairs, in plain sight of his best friends, he retreated with a sigh.

Dave stroked wisps of hair from her cheek. "You'd better head in before you catch a chill."

"As though I could have a cool molecule left on my body." She touched her lips with her fingertips. "What *was* that?"

"I think it's called a kiss." He laughed.

"Jesus. Not hardly. I've kissed plenty of guys before."

Dave frowned.

"None of them fired me up like that. Amazing."

"How about we work on it some more after the storm?"

She couldn't speak so she nodded instead.

"Call me, Kayla. Let's talk."

"Promise."

Dave pivoted and leapt down the stairs, grinning at her over his shoulder as he loped to the truck. If Neil had pressed his face any closer to the driver's side window for a peep at the exchange, he'd have left a nose print on the glass. The instant he spotted his friend approaching, he turned the key in his truck's ignition.

The powerful engine roared.

Then it sputtered.

Right before it died.

CHAPTER TWO

"How could you have checked the spark plugs so fast?"

"For the fourth time, they're fine." Neil knocked Dave away then dropped the hood with a resounding *clunk*. Six inches reduced visibility to shit considering the giant snowflakes buffeting them all.

Kayla caught the tail end of the closest thing to a brawl she'd witnessed from the men as she returned to the gathering. She'd scooted inside long enough to slip on her boots and a hoodie when she realized something had gone way wrong.

"It's probably the battery." Neil paced beside his friends. "This frigid weather could have sapped it if it were on the edge. By the time we haul Kayla's car over and jump it, plus run the engine long enough to guarantee we don't end up stranded in a snow bank halfway down the mountain, it'll be too late. This storm is nuts."

"Hell, I'm not sure leaving now would be a great idea." James scratched his chin. "This could be a blessing in disguise. It's coming harder than we expected. Driving in this would be unwise."

The three men faced her as one.

So much for a peaceful, *naked* vacation. "Come inside. You're welcome to stay."

"Are you sure…"

"Yes." Kayla grabbed Dave's hand to tug him toward the house. Neil and James shrugged then followed. She shivered despite her recent additions.

The guys shucked their boots and jackets as she headed for the kitchen. After working nearly twelve hours straight, they had to be starving in addition to cold. "What would you like for dinner? I'm guessing salted-caramel hot chocolate and Morgan's day-old spice cookies aren't going to cut it tonight."

The crew had fallen in love with her specialty beverage, spurring her to consider making it a staple at the spa. She'd brewed it for them every day at quitting time. Except today, since they'd tried to beat the storm. Tried and failed.

"You don't have to wait on us. I know you were hoping for some down time. Why don't you relax by the fire, read or do whatever it is you do in the evenings? We can fend for ourselves. Stay out of your hair." Dave approached behind her, inciting another chill.

When she trembled, he wrapped her in his heat. His strong arms banded around her, tucking her close to the furnace of his chest. She wished their offensive sweaters didn't create barriers between them. Long, thorough strokes of his broad palms infused her with warmth and dampened her pussy.

"Don't be ridiculous. This isn't exactly a mansion." She glanced around the log cabin. Open floor plans didn't allow for much privacy. A low bar separated the kitchen space from the main living area and a steep, narrow staircase led to her loft bedroom. The laundry room and extended pantry sat on the far side of her bathroom, the only truly walled-off space.

"We'll have to figure out the sleeping arrangements. You're the biggest. You should take my bed." She grimaced when she realized she couldn't accommodate them all comfortably. If she were petite, she could bunk on the chaise. At close to six feet, no one would call her dainty. Hell, James was shorter than her by a few inches and Neil only had her by a little bit. "I can fit on one couch, and I think James can manage on the loveseat but Neil—"

"Neil and James sleep together. They can have the bed." Dave didn't make a big deal of his revelation. Neither of his friends seemed to mind the sharing.

She stepped from the shelter of his hold in time to catch a glance James and Neil exchanged. They smiled at each other with a perfect combination smoky sweetness. How hadn't she guessed at their relationship before? She supposed the seamless interaction of all the guys had disguised the couple's intimacy. Could more than lifelong friendship be at play in the crew at large?

"I'll be good on the rug by the fire. That thing must be a foot deep. Don't stress." Dave grinned. "In fact, why don't you let *me* cook for *you*? This could be fun."

"Oh crap, you'd better supervise." James nudged Neil toward the kitchen. "Last time he said that he made chili so spicy I couldn't sit for a week."

Neil chuckled. He landed a playful smack on his boyfriend's ass before he joined Dave.

"Yeah, you weren't laughing then." James flung the rebuttal at his lover's back before asking her, "Are you okay with this?"

James didn't look away or fidget.

"With the three of you crashing my alone time or your love for another man?" She sensed, more than heard, the two guys in the kitchen focused on their discussion.

"Both, I suppose."

"Don't insult me. You really think I'm some kind of ass cookie?" Kayla smothered James in a bear hug. She may have been taller but his lean, muscled arms embraced her with impressive strength. She rested her cheek on his forehead, encouraging him to snuggle into her chest. "You're always welcome in my home. If anything, I'm jealous. Your boyfriend is smoking hot."

"Better watch out, James." Neil's usual teasing floated over the bar. "I think you're riling Dave. No telling what he'll put in your food if you don't take your stare off her breasts."

They both laughed as they broke apart, any trace of discomfort banished.

***

Plates piled with spaghetti and meat sauce along with a basket of garlic bread perfumed Kayla's house with savory steam. Her stomach rumbled, blocking out the sound of ice pinging off the windowpane for a moment. Snow drifted higher than her shins on the porch. Steady streams of precipitation streaked past the light post, showing no sign of stopping anytime soon.

She tugged at the waistband of her jeans when her fingers encountered the denim. Though loose, it still irritated her abdomen. James set one more bundle of wood on the floor of the laundry room before shucking his coat, unwrapping his scarf and peeling off his gloves. She wished she could undress.

He joined them at the dinner table, stomping his feet to regain circulation. "Shit, it's colder than a well digger's left ass cheek out there."

"Want me to warm you up?" Neil's crooked grin inspired a moan to slip from her parted lips.

"What's that, Kay?" Dave teased.

"I said, 'Let's eat.'"

The guys grinned, but didn't hesitate. They dug into the meal. For several minutes, silence reigned, dotted with the occasional clinks of artistic handmade silverware against heavy earthenware plates, mugs settling on the rustic table and the obnoxious beep of Dave's cell phone.

"Shit! I forgot. I had...plans." He stalked from their gathering, already hauling the device from his pocket.

Urgent whispers drifted from the far side of the cabin, where he huddled in the corner, facing away from their gathering.

Kayla dropped her fork. It clattered off her plate and skidded onto the floor. Did he have a date? Had his kiss been impulsive? Did he regret the brief collision still burning her lips? Was some other woman waiting for him—dressing up and putting on makeup in hopes of luring him into her bed after dinner and a movie?

Neil reached behind him in the cozy space to withdraw a clean utensil from the drawer on the bar. "Oops, here."

When she didn't accept his offering immediately, James patted her shoulder. "Hey, don't go there."

"Hmm?" She tried not to focus on the wisps of raspy conversation floating into the kitchen.

"It's not what you think. That didn't look good, but I'm sure there's some other explanation." James sent her a soft smile. "Dave's been knotted up over you since the moment we spied you on the porch as we pulled up for our consultation. He hasn't seen anyone…any women, since then."

Kayla swore a blush dusted James's cheeks. Could he mean…? And why was the idea so appealing to her when she wanted Dave for herself? In a matter of hours things had spiraled out of control. The howling wind couldn't counteract the heat blazing through her kitchen, igniting insanity.

"So, what do you two plan to occupy yourself with over the next few days? Sorry to say I don't even have a TV," she rambled to avoid eavesdropping on Dave.

"I think we're capable of entertaining ourselves." James winked at Neil.

"That should be interesting." Dave ambled to his place at the table, straddled the chair and resumed devouring his dinner. "I don't mind hearing, seeing...whatever. But Kayla didn't sign up for the live edition of Skinemax."

Her spine steeled. She stretched the neckband of her soft shirt, trying to ease the constriction on her throat. So now he thought her sheltered because she didn't have a Friday-night hookup to blow off? "How the hell would you know what I'm interested in? Forget voyeurism. Maybe I have guys over for foursomes all the time. Women too. Maybe I'm a freak who enjoys roaming the mountainside in the buff and hooking up with anyone who flips my switch."

"Whoa. What the hell just happened?" Dave shot glances to each of his friends as though begging for a lifeline.

"I think you pissed her off." Neil attempted to hide his smirk behind his napkin. Too bad no sauce had stained his curved lips. "Moron."

"Tell her who called." James earned a glare for his intervention. He shrugged then blew her a kiss.

"It was Joe."

"Why?" Neil tilted his head. "Did he and Mike run into trouble?"

"Nah." Dave adjusted his woven-cedar placemat. "It took longer than they hoped, but they made it home fine."

"Man, maybe you're dumber than I thought." Neil refused to drop the subject no matter how hard she concentrated on transmitting her thoughts to him.

Shut up. Shut up. Shut up.

If they guilted Dave into admitting something she couldn't erase from her memory, it'd be one hell of a long sentence for them all, confined in such close quarters until the road re-opened.

"Jesus. You'd think I kicked a puppy. Screw this." Dave shoved a couple inches from the table. "It was supposed to be a fucking secret, but it's not like you can spill the beans up here."

"About?" Neil and James leaned forward.

Kayla got the feeling they didn't often keep each other in the dark.

"Joe asked me to shop with him tonight. For a ring. An engagement ring." Dave's smile nearly blinded her. "He's planning to pop the question to Morgan next month, on Valentine's Day."

"No shit." James scrubbed his hands over his face. "Like it wasn't coming sooner or later. He might as well have asked her to marry him on Halloween. He was playing for keeps even then."

"I know." Dave shrugged. "He's still nervous for some reason."

"There's not a chance in holy hell she'll say no." Neil beamed. "Morgan's too smart to turn down her destiny. You can feel the electricity between them any time you're near. And I don't even mean the times we've..."

"What?" Kayla could have kicked herself for cutting in when their revelations stalled.

Dave scanned around the table. James and Neil nodded so subtly, she might have missed it if she hadn't stared at them with wide eyes.

"It's no secret we're great friends." Dave set his utensils on his plate and gave her his full attention. "The crew is tight. Closer than brothers. We share everything. Including sex. With women we've cared for through the years, and—"

"With each other," she finished for him. It made perfect sense.

"Yeah." Neil confirmed her suspicions.

Yum-o-licious. She squirmed in her seat. A pulse of arousal dampened her panties. "Nice. How does that work?"

"Figures." Dave laughed before reaching over to clasp her hand. She squeezed his fingers. "I debated telling you for weeks, and you're genuinely curious. No censure, no embarrassment, no disgust."

"What a high opinion you have of me." She rolled her eyes.

"It's hard to admit your kinks, no matter how sure you are someone's cool, that it's safe. It's still a giant leap of faith."

Kayla sighed as she recalled her own omission. Who was she to give him shit?

"You're right." She drew their joined hands to her lips and kissed his knuckles. "So if Morgan's aware of the crew's preferences, why is Joe worried about proposing?"

"It's dumb. He's afraid she might not accept his nature for the long haul. As if it's one thing to date and fool around, but another to marry someone, to bond with them forever, because their tastes are unconventional."

"Bullshit." Neil shook his head. "They're already fused. He couldn't pry them apart if he tried. They'd both shatter."

"Duh." Dave rocked onto the back legs of the pine chair. "I've been over this a million times with him. Part of him gets it, the rest is terrified he'll lose his soul mate. Morgan's been burned before. I think he's scared she'll bolt. Not that I agree."

Kayla peeked at him from beneath her lashes. He returned her stare as though waiting for her to weigh in. She barely resisted shoving her sleeves up her forearms. *Damn, it's hot in here.* "Sounds like Joe's freaked out over nothing. Tell me what it's like between you guys? How do things work now that Kate and Morgan are in the picture?"

"Why don't we clean up the kitchen then move this party by the fire so we can be more comfortable while we divulge our convoluted life story?" Neil suggested.

"We'll answer all of your questions." James nodded.

"Then maybe you can tell me if you're still interested in investigating the chemistry between us." Dave's murmur sent a shiver through her. "I'm dying to taste you again."

"You could be our dessert. Who needs TV?" Neil laughed when James smacked his rock-hard abs with the back of his hand. "What?"

"Behave."

"Make me."

The two men chased each other around the kitchen island, trading a few stinging spanks with a spatula and a wooden spoon before turning serious about their chores. Suds flew as Dave plunged his arms into the dishwater, scrubbing so fast a bit of the foamy liquid sloshed onto his socks.

CHAPTER THREE

The four of them snagged overstuffed husband cushions from the corner of the room and piled them on the area rug in front of the fire. They sank into the comfy cross between beanbags and pillows.

Kayla sighed, wishing she could feel the texture of the faux fur on her legs and the crinkled silk on her back. She yanked the hem of her sweater.

"What'd that thing do to you?" Dave winced then smoothed the pucker she'd made in the cornflower-blue fabric of her sweater. The caress of his hand on her trim belly made her hips jerk in his direction. If he noticed, he didn't call her out. "You're uncomfortable. Go ahead and change.

We don't mind you hanging out in your pajamas. Hell, I'd sign on for dish duty for a week if it'd net me a pair of sweats right now."

"That won't help," she grumbled.

"Why not?" James narrowed his sexy blue eyes on her.

"Because." She debated explaining, but the truth stuck in her throat. Despite their earlier confessions and their permissive views on sexuality, Dave had been right. Sharing her unusual preferences still frightened her. Too many others hadn't understood.

"You've been fidgeting with your clothes for hours." Dave stilled her fingers. They'd plucked at the seams of her jeans, which left skindentations on the sides of her thighs. "Actually, I've noticed you do it a bunch. Please tell me you're not worried about how you look. You're gorgeous."

"Thank you." She blushed. "No, it's nothing like that. I might have been self-conscious about my height, my size, when I was a teenager. Not now."

"Well, don't let us cramp your style." Neil waved at the three men. "We're fine with whatever you want to wear—holey sweats, ball gown or birthday suit. It doesn't matter to us."

"Be careful what you wish for."

"What's that supposed to mean, baby?" Dave scooted closer, taking her chin in his hand. He angled her face until she couldn't avoid his sultry eyes, which smoldered in the firelight.

She couldn't hide any longer without sacrificing her integrity. Besides, it would even their swap of secrets—seal their bond, sort of like blood brothers but hotter.

"I detest clothes," she blurted. "All clothes. I can't stand them."

Dave, James and Neil stared at her. None of them reacted.

Kayla poured out the truth she'd yearned to share for weeks. "My spa? It's not just for relaxing in the woods.

I'm opening a clothing-optional facility. A place where naturists can come to indulge without worrying about others judging them. Someplace sheltered, beautiful and high-quality for like-minded individuals to enjoy a break from their daily routines."

She waited for the crew to laugh.

They didn't.

"That's a damn bit more interesting than a frou-frou spa." Dave smiled. "Sounds like a brochure when you pitch it. I can picture it. It's a great idea."

"With you in charge, it'll be a huge success." James rested a hand on her knee, where it tucked near his hip.

"So are you... What'd you call it?" Neil waggled his eyebrows. "A naturist?"

"Damn straight." She folded her arms across her chest.

"Then what the hell are we doing sitting around in our work clothes?" Dave unbuttoned his fly. "Do you have any idea how stiff and scratchy these are? I'm roasting with this freaking bonfire too."

"Wait!" Kayla covered his broad fingers with her smaller ones. Bad move. The bulge of his erection flexed beneath their joined hands. "Don't."

"Why not?" James raised an eyebrow at her.

"You're screwing me up. All three of you." She bounded to her feet, yanking on the roots of her waist-length copper hair. "You suck."

"Mmm." Neil moaned. "James and Dave do a respectable job. It's not really my thing, though."

"*Respectable*?" James flipped Neil off. "That's not what you said this morning."

"Guys." Dave shushed their squabbling before it escalated into a wrestling match. "Calm down a minute. What's wrong, Kay?"

She flinched when he brushed her hair aside to lay one palm on her shoulder. Her stomach did somersaults, begging her to pivot in his hold and steal another sample of his luscious mouth. How strong would the craving be if they were actually nude?

Undeniable.

"I've spent a large part of my life trying to explain my beliefs to others. Ignorant people will often confuse nudism with some kind of contagious, immoral hedonism. They assume because you're naked, you intend to fuck anything that moves—willing or not. As if you'll lure innocents to the dark side with bare skin. Sure... I'm open about my sexuality. I enjoy intimacy with the right man, woman or a combination thereof, but that doesn't mean I'm some kind of slut—"

"Stop right there." Dave cupped her other shoulder then pressed, gentle but insistent, until she pivoted. "You weren't really teasing at dinner, were you? Your belief in naturism does not make you some kind of dirty leper, driving you to roam around the mountain naked, fucking anything you encounter. We would never believe such bullshit. How could you imagine we would after what we told you about our relationship?"

"Because this time it's true." A tear slipped from the corner of her eye, horrifying her. She dashed it away before it'd traveled an inch across her cheek.

Dave reached out.

Kayla stepped back, evading his comforting embrace. "During sessions where I'm around you naked—any of you, all of you—sex eclipses everything else in my mind. The whole time I massage you, I wonder what it'd be like to have you buried inside me. I want to ride you. I'd give half this mountain to taste you. I'm *dying* for you to use me."

Dave groaned.

"When I need to be strong and sure in my purpose, you've given me reason to doubt." She slumped. Holding her frame upright a moment longer seemed impossible. "Maybe I was kidding myself all along. Maybe it's impossible to separate nudity from sexuality."

"So, you're saying you're only attracted to me—to us—when we're undressed?" Dave crowded closer.

"Ah, no." She shook her head as she took stock of the ache between her legs and the heavy weight of her sensitive breasts. "But when you're bare, the magnetism's impossible to resist. It's not like that when you're covered up."

"Are you lying to us...or to yourself? Consider carefully or I'll prove you're a little fibber."

"How?" She gave herself a mental head slap. Why antagonize the man? *Because you're tired of wanting and not having. Tired of restraint.*

"Take off your clothes." Dave's command weakened her knees. "Do it quick, or I'll rip them to shreds so you never have to worry about wearing them again."

"Oh shit, now you did it." James shifted his gaze between her and Dave.

Kayla shrugged. No matter what happened, it would be a welcome relief. She shimmied her jeans off her hips without unfastening them then whipped her sweater over her head as she kicked the denim so hard it flopped over the armrest of the couch. She rolled her shoulders and stretched. Finally.

Though she forced herself to don the necessary garments, she never could torture herself with a bra or underwear. Naked, she propped one hand on her hip and stared down the three prime males fixated on her every move.

Dave breathed in and out several times, his fingers clenched at his sides as he took in the smattering of bright, floral tattoos decorating her ribs and the modest silver hoops piercing her nipples. The metal tugged deliciously as her flesh reacted to his appraisal. "Lie on the rug between James and Neil."

Her body complied without conscious approval from her mind. Something about this man, these men, called to her on an instinctive level.

"I love it when he turns all bossy." Neil hummed his approval.

"Good 'cause you're about to assist." Dave doled out orders as she sank to floor.

Soft and fuzzy, the rug caressed her backside from her calves to her ass to her shoulders while allowing air to circulate over her skin. She squirmed, relishing the sensation while the fire cooked one side of her front and the cool air in the room regulated the other. Freedom sang through her blood with each pump of her racing heart.

Kayla surrendered to instinct, spreading her legs to tease the three men ringing her with the glistening fluid on her upper thighs. She painted the proof of her arousal over her waxed pussy with the tip of one finger, biting her lip when she skimmed her clit.

No one had ever dared to call her inhibited.

"Jesus." Neil untucked his shirt.

"No." Dave placed a restraining hand on the other man's tense forearm. "Leave your clothes on. Every stitch. We're going to make her scream. Blow her mind. Steal all her rational thought without showing a hint of skin."

"Fuck." James dropped to his knees beside her shoulder. She reached out to take his proffered hand, lacing their fingers.

"You win." Kayla could care less about her moral dilemma at the moment. For now, it would be enough to erase the lust hazing her mind so she could think clearly about the issue in the aftermath of great sex. "I understand. No need for some great lesson. Just don't leave me like this."

"Oh, we're not about to abandon you." Dave situated himself on his haunches between her knees, opening them wider with one massive hand on each of her thighs. "This isn't at all how I planned to do this, but I'd be lying if I said the end result was much different. I want you. I want to share you, give you three times the pleasure I could myself."

"Mmm." She tried to generate an intelligent answer. Instead, her hips responded for her, rising to meet his roving fingers as they teased along her legs to stroke her smooth mound. Never one to sit passive and wait for her lover to take charge, she urged him closer.

"Keep her still." Dave barked the order to his friends, who didn't hesitate.

Neil joined them on the rug, grasping her wrist and pinning it to the floor beside her head. James followed suit.

The rustle of their jeans as they shifted sent butterflies racing through her abdomen. Something about the contrast seemed decadent. It amplified her joy at being nude. Rough grazes from the fabric shielding the men's legs had her breath wheezing double time.

Dave leaned forward, bracing himself on bulging forearms on either side of her head. He smiled as he observed her potent longing up close and personal before covering her lips with his. He explored with the tip of his tongue, teasing at the corner of her mouth until she relented and granted him entrance. They played—tickling, taunting, tempting—for long minutes, until neither had the breath to continue without passing out.

James squeezed her hand when she whimpered.

"You drive me crazy too, Kay," Dave whispered as he nipped her lip. "Just so you know."

Neil grunted. "No shit. How many trips down this mountain have we had to listen you ramble on and on about how smoking she is?"

"Am I wrong?" Dave lifted an eyebrow.

"Fuck no." Neil's lips quirked. "But you're still as annoying as an itchy nose when your hands are covered in drywall dust."

"I guess we know who's getting off last." James laughed. "Focus, boys. Kayla's on the edge."

"Not so easy. We can push her much further." Dave winked at James. "You were too busy fondling her to notice her reaction to your announcement earlier. I think she likes the idea of two guys together. Don't you, baby?"

"I support gay rights, yes." She salvaged the destruction of her rationality long enough to respond. "Everyone should live and love however makes them happy as far as I'm concerned."

"It was more than that, but I'll give it to you for now." Dave shifted his focus to James. He planted one hand on the back of his partner's neck and navigated their journey.

If the couple hadn't still restrained her, she would have touched herself while the guys shared a remarkably tender kiss.

"My turn." Neil cut in, devouring Dave's mouth for several seconds before reaching for his lover. The instant Neil and James meshed, Kayla could tell the difference. Friendship and shared sensual escapades had nothing on true love. The men stared into each other's eyes as they connected, letting their souls speak to one another.

She sighed.

"Pretty awesome, right?" Dave nodded at her.

The two men broke apart, panting. They faced to her together, both sporting wicked grins. They descended in unison, each laving the tip of one of her breasts. Her eyes rolled in their sockets when they tugged on the jewelry there before angling their heads for another taste of each other.

The alternating stimulation captivated her attention. Her eyes dried out from refusing to blink as the guys worshipped her chest, then each other, over and over. She almost forgot Dave, until he moved, settling deeper in the vee of her thighs. He lay on the floor between her legs, nibbling a trail from her knee toward her pussy.

She would have begged them to allow her to admire their fantastic bodies, touch them, if she could have found her voice. Neil bit lightly on her nipple, causing her to squirm. A trickle of arousal escaped her clenching pussy.

"Oh, what's this?" Dave mocked her. "I thought you only wanted us 'cause our hot naked bodies triggered some kind of naturism fetish?"

He swiped a finger through her engorged folds, collecting the damning evidence. He sucked the digit clean, groaning at her taste before swiping another sample to feed to James. The other man paused his attentions to her breast to savor the flavor of the ecstasy they inspired.

"She's delicious," he groaned before kissing Neil once more, sharing the mingled taste of all four of them.

Dave held her gaze as he replaced his finger at her opening. His hooded eyes turned glassy as he penetrated her tight rings of muscle with a slow, steady invasion. She cried out as her body hugged him, inciting a riot of pleasure that burned her from the inside out.

James whispered in her ear as Neil licked her belly with soothing strokes. The shirt covering his broad shoulders scraped her waist. "Your reaction to us has nothing to do with our clothing or lack thereof. Don't confuse the two."

She quaked as a precursor to orgasm rolled through her. The initial joining of their bodies thrilled her. James traced the dark outline of a delicate vine, which snaked up her side and across the underside of her breast, with his tongue. "So pretty."

"She likes that," Dave rasped when her tissue fluttered around his embedded finger. He lifted his chin toward Neil. "Feel for yourself."

Kayla expected Dave to withdraw, vacating the moist heat of her pussy to leave room for his friend. Instead, he paused the tiny nudges rocking his finger within her clinging sheath while Neil aligned his hand for the optimum approach.

Neil lifted his talented mouth from her breast to nibble her neck. She tensed when the heel of his palm settled on her mound and a broad finger tunneled beside Dave's, snaking beyond the initial resistance of her core.

The men stretched her boundaries and her body. Despite her earlier bravado, she'd never experienced something so intense, so wild or so decadent.

"Damn, she's hot." Neil claimed her lips less gently as her desire infected him. The weight of his full erection branded her hip.

He curled his finger inside her, caressing the ultra-sensitive front wall of her pussy with a circular motion that jostled him against Dave.

Wet smacks accompanied their joint explorations.

Kayla squeezed James's hand when he suspended his stroking on her side and breast, demanding his attention.

"Sorry, Kay." His harsh exhalation buffeted her damp nipple. "They distracted me. I wish I could feel how soft you are. How lush."

"Do it." Dave growled. "She'll surrender with all three of us inside her. Together."

The idea alone had rapture rippling the walls of her pussy. Neil adjusted his hand so a calloused pad jolted her clit, granting her a chance to regain control.

"Not yet," Dave insisted as he supervised. "Wait for James. I mean, I know you only want us when we're naked—"

"Shut up." She snarled as a blush crept up her chest.

He laughed and screwed his finger deeper, driving her insane. "Hurry, James."

The third man glanced at her and she couldn't stop the plea that burst from her chest. "Please. Join them."

James nuzzled their noses as he walked his fingers between her breasts and over her softly rounded abdomen. He layered his hand partially over Neil's. The other half rested on her skin, a thin sheen of perspiration adhering their bodies.

He traced his finger beside Neil's, trapping her clit gently between their hands. She groaned and tried to rub against them. No matter how she fidgeted, she couldn't generate enough friction to satisfy her longing.

Her mind blanked when James pushed into her soaked pussy. The wiggling of three independent intruders drove her insane.

"Help me."

James and Neil resumed their play at her breasts.

"Why? Do you want us? Even though we're fully dressed?" Dave spoke through gritted teeth.

"Yes!"

His smile looked more like a grimace. He dove between her legs, lapping at her clit and his friends' hands with sloppy passes of his soft tongue. Colors streamed through her vision. She focused on the sweet ache expanding in her pelvis. She tried to harness the power of the moment, ride it forever.

She didn't stand a chance.

Tremors built rapidly into irrepressible waves of desire. She threw her head back and shouted as she came around the three thrusting, massaging, spreading fingers that exported every last shred of rapture from the explosion. Dave hummed as he suckled her clit, extending the wash of contentment suffusing her being.

When the men exited her body, one by one, she peeled her eyelids open. James and Neil held their hands out toward each other. Neil inserted his long finger between his lover's parted lips. James licked, slurped and swallowed until Neil retracted the treat. James returned the favor.

She shivered with the aftershocks of delight.

The metallic rip of a zipper unknitting caught her attention. She flicked her gaze to Dave, who extracted his long, thick cock from the fly of his jeans. The flushed, veined shaft contrasted starkly with his otherwise clad form as he took it in hand. She licked her lips.

"Not this time, baby." He grunted as the ridge of his knuckles passed over the dripping head. "I think our guys here deserve a reward don't you?"

She reached out to place a hand on James and Neil's nearest thighs as they knelt on either side of her, finally realizing they'd freed her wrists. "Definitely."

"James loves to watch a guy shoot his come. Cleaning up the evidence never fails to set him off. Want to see?"

"God, yes." She cupped her breasts, pressing the tender mounds together as she imagined warm spray icing the tips. But why stop at one man? She reached to either side of her, fumbling in the general direction of James and Neil's veiled erections. They got the hint.

Within seconds, they'd made quick work of the fastenings on their jeans and arranged themselves so their cocks protruded, pointing toward her receptive torso. She couldn't help herself—her fingers sought their steely flesh. She moaned when she compared the weight and feel of them. James, so stiff it had to hurt. Neil, longer and thicker, though no more eager than his lover, who pounded into her fist when she didn't move fast enough to suit him.

Dave grinned down at her. "That's right, Kay. They can't take much more. Where do you want their come?"

She tipped their cocks, aiming them at her breasts.

"Shit, yeah." Neil pumped through the circle of her fingers, damp with the precome he'd coated them with. His pelvis knocked into the ring formed by the side of her palm with several quick, hard thrusts. The definition of the ridge at his tip increased, impressing her with the transformation. His shouted warning of impending release was completely unnecessary.

His balls drew tight to his body as though trying to force their way out of his cock. The first jets of silky fluid overshot their target, landing partially on her far breast. The remainder decorated James's thigh. The man didn't seem to mind.

James groaned and joined his lover, painting her with his come. Splatters of hot fluid seared her skin, which looked more olive compared to the pearly white stands draping over her nipple rings and the colorful blossoms of her tattoos. Neil still twitched in her hold when James dropped lower to capture the last of Neil's orgasm on his tongue.

He ingested their mingled release before it had a chance to cool on her skin. The intoxicating sight couldn't monopolize her attention for long, though, when Dave leaned his hips forward, pressing his cock to her belly with one heavy hand. He thrust into the friction he created, making several long passes as James continued to shudder, intent on cleaning her torso.

The motion of Dave's cock rubbed his balls over her clit, inciting a flash of ecstasy to rejuvenate from the embers of her satisfaction. The dilation of his pupils sealed her fate. That much hunger would be impossible to deny. They rode the final wave of shared rapture together.

Her hips rocked, stroking him as his cock pulsed. The first blast of his semen landed on James's cheek. The man moaned then lunged, mouth open, tongue extended, to catch the remainder of Dave's gift. Kayla stared as her insides shivered, drowning her in wave after wave of pleasure.

Dave slumped, his shoulders heaving as he relaxed between her legs. James leaned closer to suck the last drop of fluid from the tip of Dave's cock before tucking the softening tool back into Dave's jeans and zipping him up. He patted the placket with a contented grin that elicited a moan from Dave.

Neil's reverent curse shifted her attention. He, too, towered over her, fully dressed once more. By the time she returned her wide-eyed stare to James, he'd also hidden himself from her view. Damn them.

"Ready to admit your attraction has nothing to do with naturism?" Dave's soft tone didn't rub her face in her earlier refusal to believe in the amazing opportunity she'd been given. In fact, his question sounded more like a plea.

"Yes." She reached out, taking his hand and using it to pull him over her until she could cover his face in light kisses. "It's all about you. Clothes or not."

"Ahem." Neil cleared his throat with a ridiculous, exaggerated noise.

"Okay, all of you." She giggled. "Thank you."

Neil ruffled her hair, then groaned as he regained his feet. He trundled off to the bathroom. James followed, granting her and Dave a moment alone.

"Things don't have to go any further—with them or without—if that's not what you have in mind." His throat flexed as she considered her response.

"And if I want things to go a hell of a lot further?"

"Thank God."

CHAPTER FOUR

ayla and Dave emerged from the shower together to find Neil and James cuddled on the floor, a stack of board games nearby. She smiled when they met her gaze—all four of them completely nude. Nothing seemed different than before, other than the lack of constriction she'd suffered beneath the weight of her clothes.

The three men took naturism to a new level. Their honed bodies paid homage to the human form. Comfortable and confident, they lounged in various levels of arousal. Dave wrapped his arms around her from behind, rooting his face in her damp hair. The erection he hadn't permitted her to soothe in the steamy mist of her bathroom nudged her lower back.

"Save it for later," he'd murmured when she rubbed against him like a cat beneath the relaxing spray that cleaned the last of their sticky pleasure from her chest and belly. He'd proven he had a hell of a lot more control than she did. *Yum.*

"Up for a game?" James disrupted her train of thought before she could rotate in Dave's arms and steal what she needed. To hell with savoring the anticipation.

"I rule at Yahtzee." Neil grinned.

"What are you? Eighty?" James poked his lover in the ribs.

"I thought about recommending Twister, but...that's a little predictable, don't you think?"

They all laughed as Kayla and Dave settled opposite from the pair.

"How about Trivial Pursuit?" Dave suggested.

"It's my favorite." She sighed as she reclined against him. His arm encircled her torso, resting beneath her breasts. He didn't try to fondle her or take advantage of the placement. The easy contentment made her heart soar even as her pussy moistened.

"Done." He smiled at her. "We can be a team. As long as you're okay with the orange thinger. I'm always the orange one."

"Sounds good to me." She lifted her smile to his for a quick kiss before unpacking the pieces and setting up the board.

Hours flew by as they won, lost, rematched and laughed their asses off like kids discovering fun for the first time. At ease, she didn't realize she sat, cross-legged, bald pussy completely exposed, until Neil's stare lingered a little too long. She teased him by trailing her fingertips over the soft swell between her legs.

"You like my tattoo?" She traced the artistic squiggles of the abstract design where it flirted with her mons.

"Oh yeah, he's a real art connoisseur." James laughed then slapped Neil on the back of the head with a playful tap.

"More like a lover of all beauty." Neil bit James's lip. His half-hard cock plumped where it rested on his thigh. "There's a lot of eye candy in this room."

"No kidding." Kayla didn't mind him looking. "A little skewed on the male side, though."

"Uh." Dave cleared his throat. "You said something about that before. Are you bi, Kay?"

"I'm not a big fan of labels. I do what feels right in the moment and don't worry about what outsiders would call it." She shrugged. "I've been with girls before, sure. Would I be again? Yep, if it was someone I felt a connection to. Is it something I have to have to be happy long term? Not if the person, or people, I'm with satisfy me."

"I couldn't have said that better myself." Neil beamed at her. "It's like we were meant to find you. This past year has sealed my belief in fate."

"How so?" She tilted her head as she studied him.

"I guess I always worried the crew's friendship had a life expectancy." He flicked an imaginary piece of lint from his leg before looking to Dave and James.

"What the fuck, Neil?" Dave glared at the other man. "You've never said anything about that. We won't lose each other. We're too much a part of one another."

"Yeah, but I also understand what it's like to love someone until you can't believe it's real." He locked his fingers with James's. "There's no walking away from that pull. I figured when it happened to you guys, you'd have to pick one or the other. The girl or the group."

James nodded. "I can see that. I wish you'd shared your worries with me."

"I knew, no matter what, I'd always have you." Neil sighed. "How could I tell you my fears without making it seem like that isn't enough? Like you're not everything?"

Kayla glanced away, feeling for the first time like an intruder.

"Shhh." James climbed into Neil's lap and soothed his lover with gentle kisses. "How many times have I told you I get it? You love me. When I watch you fuck a woman, or mess around with the crew, I can tell it's not the same as what you feel when you make love to me. You care for them. You respect them and please them. You take what you need from them, but you *love* me. I never doubt that."

Their connection acted as the biggest turn-on of her life. Kayla didn't realize she'd covered her aching breast with her fingers, tugging on the silver hoop in her nipple, until Dave blanketed her hand with his own and took up where she'd begun. He paused long enough to situate her in his lap, her back to his ripped chest so they could bask in the magic before them.

"The idea makes you hot, doesn't it? You're curious." His breath teased the edge of her ear.

"Mmm. Yes." She squirmed in Dave's hold, his hands sliding from her chest to her waist to keep her in place on his lap. They continued to descend until he cupped her mound in plain view of his friends, who'd focused on her and Dave once more. She didn't object. The weight of his hard-on pressed the small of her back, the tip painting a moist trail there.

"Would you like them to show you the bond between them?" He whispered, "They're fucking amazing together. They love each other so much it makes the sex ten times steamier."

Dave's open acceptance thrilled her. Finally a man who didn't seem threatened by indulging their shared needs, wherever the pursuit might lead. Nothing could have been more attractive.

"Yes. Please." Witnessing Neil and James's affection would rank as a high honor.

Neil smiled as he turned to his lover. He cupped James's face in his palms as though the slighter man were made of glass. They melded together, beginning with their lips. Soon their bodies pressed tight, chest-to-chest, thighs tangled, cock on cock.

Proud.

Vulnerable.

Gorgeous.

Neil directed their encounter, gifting his partner with as much rapture as he could. They traded nips, licks and glides of their lips. Intense focus didn't allow for anything else in the world to register on their passion.

But Dave couldn't miss her escalating desire. She ground her ass against his shaft, stroking his hard-on where it nestled in the furrow between her cheeks.

In an instant, the world shifted around her.

Dave bore her to the floor in front of the fire, nestled on her side on the thick faux-fur rug. He snugged tight behind her, spooning her, pillowing her head on his bunched biceps to preserve her view. His other hand played across the exposed skin of her abdomen, as well as the curve of her hip and ass, driving her insane. She moaned loudly, drawing the attention of all three men.

Kayla arranged her legs, draping her top thigh over Dave's hip, granting him free access.

But it wasn't the man holding her who accepted the invitation.

James looked to Neil, who nodded.

"Can I taste you?" James separated from his lover and crawled to her, his gaze fixating on the shimmering arousal coating her pussy, beginning to trickle onto her thigh.

She tipped her head toward Dave.

"No, baby. It's not my choice. He's asking you." Dave reached between her legs to paint her juices across the softness of her inner thighs with the barest of touches. She needed more. "Whatever you like. No doubts. No jealousy. Take what you need. Give what you can. We all know where we stand here."

Did she know? What was she to them but an opportunistic fuck? Did she care at the moment? No. A chance to explore like this didn't come around every day.

Their intimacy was a gift.

She stretched until she could entwine her fingers in James's hair to guide him closer. He made quick work of cleaning Dave's fingers then groaned as he skimmed her mound. When his tongue peeked out to swipe through her slit, circling her clit before making another circuit, they both moaned.

Neil lay on his side behind his mate, holding the man eating her pussy with the same sheltering embrace Dave enfolded her in. All four of them lounged together now, Dave and her with their heads toward the fireplace, James and Neil toasting their toes, each couple facing inward toward the other.

The bundle of limbs and torsos grew denser as she thrust her pelvis toward James's talented mouth and he sidled closer, his abdomen nestled against the subtle swell made by her modest breasts. She undulated against him, enjoying the feel of skin on skin.

Behind her, Dave pursued. He tucked nearer the entire length of her, impressing her again with his extraordinary height. It wasn't often a man could make her seem diminutive.

"Damn, you have some sexy legs, Kay." Neil stroked along her thigh to her knee. "Long and thin, but toned. I'd love to have them wrapped around me while I sank into your softness."

Her pussy contracted, forcing a fresh wave of moisture onto her labia. James buried his face to reach all of the honey. The motion eliminated any remaining gap between them. His hips landed near her face, enticing her with his rock-hard erection, close enough to lick.

"Go ahead." Dave encouraged her impulse. "Suck him, baby. Show him what a good job he's doing between those pretty legs."

The wet smoothness of James's tongue slid farther back. When Dave cursed in her ear, she assumed the man holding her had received a reward for the suggestion. "Careful, James. I'm on the edge. Let me last."

Suspicion confirmed.

Ecstasy rioted in her mind. The close hold of three men, their skilled manipulation of her willing body and their open-minded quest for pleasure combined into a potent concoction. She was drunk on it after a few tiny sips.

Kayla opened her mouth, allowing James's cock—perfectly aligned—to slip inside. She laved the head in welcome as he pushed deeper within her grasp. His erection made a comfortable mouthful, astonishing her with its hardness and searing heat rather than its sheer size—unlike the ample shaft prodding her spine.

Spice melted over her taste buds. She peeked between James's legs as she sucked gently, in time to the swirl of his tongue over her sensitive opening and the swollen knot of her clit. Behind him, Neil's heavily veined cock throbbed insistently.

"You lucky bastard." Neil chuckled into his boyfriend's ear.

"Want to really blow their minds, baby?" Dave kissed her cheek. He ran his tongue around the edge of her lips, circling the base of his friend's cock with the tip.

"Hmm." Her assent caused James to jerk in her hold.

"Give him to me for a minute."

She blinked, not understanding.

"Release him."

James whimpered in protest when she pulled off his hard-on with a slurp, but he never paused in his devotion. Delirious with desire, she rocked until his mouth landed in the perfect position. The first signs of orgasm fizzled through her belly. She would have warned the men but, just then, Dave lunged forward to capture James's erection.

Neil cradled closer as his partner's hips jerked forward. The adjustment presented Neil's cock within reach of her mouth. She strained her neck until her lips wrapped around the head of his cock. Caught off guard, he bucked, driving several inches deeper. She choked.

Dave mumbled something unintelligible around James's cock. He stroked her flank, calming her. When she recovered, she stretched once more, reclaiming her tasty treat.

Catching on, Neil assisted by raising James's hips several inches in his strong grasp, aligning them all in the optimal position. She humped James's face as much as she could in the cramped arrangement. All that mattered was chasing the spears of sensation he launched into her center. Ragged gasps and unending moans surrounded her, setting her off. Her pussy tightened then exploded before she could fully enjoy the decadent tension invading her inner core.

"Yes, baby," Dave growled in her ear. "Come all over his face. Enjoy it. There's more where that came from. So much more."

Rekindled hope replaced her disappointment. The men paused, but only to shift slightly. James angled his head to kiss his partner, sharing the flavor of her climax. Neil's fingers pressed against her saturated folds, scooping generous portions of her come onto his digits. Before she could return to sanity long enough to wonder at his intentions, he slathered the fresh lubrication over James's exposed asshole. She watched from her front row seat as Neil primed his lover.

"I'd kill to fill you right now, Kayla," Dave groaned in her ear as the two lovers prepared to bond before her eyes. "No condoms, though. Damn it."

"I'm on the pill. Healthy." Hunger still clawed at her soul. She wanted to join these exceptional men. Had to be part of their joy. Coming alone hadn't fulfilled her craving. "Please."

"I'm clean too. I swear," Dave rasped. "Are you sure, baby?"

"Yes. Yes!" She shouted when he shifted a fraction of an inch and the blunt head of his cock notched in the entrance of her pussy. Her still-clenching muscles kissed his tip.

Meanwhile, Neil fit himself to his lover's opening.

While each stared at the cock of the man opposite him, Neil and Dave thrust in time, tunneling a fraction of an inch into their partners. As if by tacit agreement, Kayla and James resumed their oral explorations simultaneously. Kayla forced herself to keep her lids open though they threatened to slam closed with every talented swipe of James's tongue and every nudge of Dave's thick cock stretching her channel.

Inside her. She finally had him inside her.

Oh shit. Sex had never felt so explosive, so natural or so right.

Effortless.

Her body climbed inexorably toward completion so fast she thought her heart might implode under the pressure of being fucked while another man licked her with exquisite tenderness. She couldn't say if it were her or James who whimpered when both men bottomed out at the limits of their reach within their gracious hosts.

Rings of muscle clenched around Dave, drawing a soft curse from his lips. He burrowed his face into the crook of her neck, licking, biting and kissing as he began to move within her. His cock stroked along the swollen tissue of her pussy, caressing where she needed contact most.

James's cock spilled precome onto her tongue steadily while Neil glided in and out of his lover's stretched hole. She followed her instincts, reaching up to tease Neil's balls, needing them all to shatter together. Experience together.

Dave and Neil synchronized the crescendoing tempo of their hips, which pounded into her and James in an undeniable rhythm. Each tap of Dave's pelvis on her ass jolted her body forward, driving James's cock deeper into her mouth. The mirrored thrust of

Neil's hard-on pressed James's tongue to her clit.

Her toes curled as she attempted to resist the sparks that lit up all of her nerve endings. She whimpered in desperation when she realized no hope remained. She couldn't help but drown in the sensations these three men manufactured.

"Don't fight it, baby." Dave panted as he shuttled faster between her legs. His thick cock rubbed all the right places.

"We're here." Neil groaned as the smack of his tight abs on James's ass reverberated in her ears. "We're with you."

"Let go," Dave demanded as he bit her shoulder at the base of her neck.

The first jet of James's come may have graced the back of her throat a fraction of a second before she shattered. She couldn't say for sure.

Kayla drank the salty spray as she exploded around Dave's bulging cock.

He filled her with pulse after pulse of semen before her wild gyration tore him loose. The final spurts of his release flew from his broad tip outside of her body. The dismay ripping through her at the loss evaporated while she watched the base of Neil's shaft throb as it delivered his come from his tight, wrinkled sac into the depths of his lover's body.

Kayla lay gasping in Dave's hold, suffering the aftershocks of her orgasm for long, lingering minutes. When the men finally roused, James and Neil flipped over so they all lay the same direction, eye to eye.

Dave's weak chuckle bounced his chest against her shoulders. "Sorry 'bout that, guys."

Both Neil and James sported a partial mustache from the stray blasts of Dave's come. They looked at each other with matching, devilish smirks. Another round of contractions wrung her pussy when the men took turns licking the delicacy from each other. They shared the taste of Dave with gentle, though heated, kisses.

She angled her mouth toward Dave, who treated her to the same affectionate exchange. She couldn't say how long they made out before he nipped her bottom lip and nudged her jaw. She faced the sleepy stares of Neil and James.

Without thought, she closed the gap between them then kissed James. Soft, sweet and with no trace of awkwardness. Then she moved on to Neil, thanking him for the glorious gift they'd bestowed. The blended flavor of the three men rushed to her head.

She wilted in Dave's hold, utterly relaxed, and observed through half-closed eyes as he shared an equally intimate kiss with both men. The way their lips merged with practiced familiarity guaranteed they'd indulged in the extravagance before.

"I hope it snows forever," she mumbled before drifting off.

CHAPTER FIVE

Sunlight stabbed through the giant windows, sparkling off the icy blanket of snow that covered the mountainside in a million dazzling lights—beautiful and impossible to sleep through. Kayla snuggled into the broad, muscular chest pillowing her cheek.

She grinned at Dave's soft snoring. Damn straight, she'd worn his ass out.

The orgasms she'd succumbed to last night had been the most powerful of her life. She couldn't wait to duplicate the pleasure. Would it be possible or had novelty driven the sensations?

Kayla squirmed as she imagined taking all three men, maybe more than one at a time. Each would come deep within her, proving she could please them too. Her rocking hips encountered the bulge of Dave's magnificent erection.

She blinked then grinned as she devised a plan.

"Good morning," Neil whispered to her from his place on the pile of cushions in front of the hearth. He and James wound together. The four of them, who'd slept together like a pile of puppies, generated enough heat to keep the chill at bay despite the ashes lying where the fire had blazed. Neil reached over James. His hand spanned her shoulders, spreading warmth down her spine as he stroked her back.

James shifted to smile up at her and Dave. "Go ahead. Make his day."

She hesitated. What if their liaison last night had been just another pastime to the man beneath her, an outlet for consenting adults to entertain themselves when board games lost their luster? For the first time in a long time, maybe ever, she craved more than mutual gratification.

James smoothed the corner of her grimace. "There's nothing to worry about, Kay. He'll love every minute. Nothing's changed between last night and now."

"I think *I* might have." She leaned into James and Neil's reassuring touches. "This is more than physical. It matters. I don't really do relationships. I'm pretty sure this isn't how you start one. What if I'm screwing everything up?"

"Don't you dare doubt yourself." Neil tugged a stray lock of her hair. "Take what you need. I think you'll find it's what he wants too."

"Should Neil and I go upstairs?" James ignored his lover's glare.

"No. Stay." She drew a deep breath when Neil's fingers clenched on her back.

James and Neil supported her with strong grips as she clambered to wobbly knees. James slid his hand into the gap between her and Dave to stroke the last of the necessary steel into Dave's morning wood. Neil trailed his fingertips down her spine, through the valley of her ass to her swollen pussy. She shivered, barely containing her moan when he pushed two fingers inside as James readied Dave.

Satisfied, James pointed Dave's cock toward her moist opening. Neil withdrew his fingers and painted the excess arousal over her tight ass. He left his hand in place, idle, while she fit the opening of her pussy over the plump head of Dave's hard-on, which James supported.

"He's huge." She gasped as she sank onto the intrusion. Each fraction of an inch lower stretched her pussy wider and wider until a delicious burn radiated from her core. Cradling him inside her while he slept seemed equally naughty and divine. His body responded to her on an instinctual level none of them could deny.

"No kidding." James ran one finger around Dave's cock, testing the fit.

The tip nudged into her channel, making her pant.

"When he fucks my ass, I swear it feels like a phone pole." James sighed. "He's always gentle though. Until I can relax. Once I accommodate him, he enjoys pounding me as much as I love taking it."

She moaned at the flicker of fantasy that played through her imagination. Her muscles tensed around Dave, hugging him tighter. Last night, too much had distracted her from admiring the way they locked together. He filled her to capacity. Exactly right.

"Have you ever had anal sex, Kay?" Neil resumed his tentative massage of her back passage. He paused every few seconds to gather more natural lubrication from the junction of her and

Dave's bodies. The surplus fluid from her pussy cooled her sensitive skin even as Neil inflamed it.

"A couple times." She sighed as he teased her. Wonder blossomed at the sensation, adding to the thrill of Dave's cock impaling her bit by bit. "It wasn't that good."

"I bet that had more to do with the guys you were with than the act itself." Neil's manipulation grew more insistent. The tip of his finger probed her ass. "Would you try it again?"

"With one of the crew? Yes." She panted when it became difficult to catch her breath. James captured her hips in his hands and situated her so Dave's cock tunneled farther along her channel. She smothered him as Neil drew circles on the inside edge of her anus.

His finger popped loose when Dave shifted beneath them. "Hmmm."

He groaned, but didn't regain full consciousness.

"Lean forward." Neil's free hand pressed between her shoulders.

James stared as she bent in half. She couldn't resist a taste of Dave's parted lips.

Kayla licked him, turning his sexy mouth glossy. When she nibbled the bottom of his jaw, tension infused his relaxed limbs. Her name spilled from his lips as his eyes opened. He squinted against the overpowering sunlight.

"Am I dead?" Dave whispered into the hushed intimacy of the room.

James laughed out loud. "She looks like an angel and fucks like the devil, but no, you're just fine. Dumbass."

She held her breath as she waited for his reaction. Had she gone too far?

"Jesus, I'm fucking you." He scrubbed his face as best he could with one hand. James plastered to his side, preventing the other one from budging.

"No, *she's* definitely fucking *you*." Neil kissed her shoulder, then her neck, inspiring her to move without conscious thought.

Her pussy sucked and stroked Dave's shaft.

"Holy shit, she is." Dave's abdomen went rock hard beneath her. He lifted his hips to meet her pussy, which bussed his pelvis and the top of his scrotum. "Are you sure I'm not in heaven?"

This time she couldn't stop herself. She covered his mouth with hers, drawing on his tongue, which he thrust between her lips. Her hands landed over hard pecs, kneading the bulk there. When Neil's finger returned, covered in more of her slick juice, she nearly choked.

"What's going on back there?" Dave growled, more alert by the second. "James, is your guy getting fresh with my girl?"

"Sure is." James lifted his head to note Neil's progress. "I'm surprised you can't feel him yet."

"There he is." Dave and Kayla moaned together when Neil drove his finger into her tight ass. Dave's skull knocked on the rug-covered hardwood when he could no longer hold his head up. The slight discomfort dissolved in seconds. Dave kept talking. "He's rubbing my cock through her ass. Son of a bitch."

James glided his hand down his lithe torso, headed for his cock.

"No." Kayla flung out her wrist to stop him.

When both James and Dave stared at her like she was crazy, she laughed. "Gimme."

"Greedy, Kay." Dave thrust upward, fucking her so deep, so strong, the angle of their position rocked her world. "I like that. Tell him where you want him."

"In my mouth." She didn't hesitate for an instant. "Yours, too. It drove me insane when you sucked his cock."

Neil bit her right cheek then added a second finger to his act. "Fuck, yeah. I can't wait to see it as I introduce my cock to your ass."

"Either you should hurry or we should hold off a minute on the blow-jobbing." James surrendered a nervous chuckle. "Despite last night, I don't think I can take much more."

"I won't rush this." Neil spread his fingers in her ass, opening her passage a little wider. "I'm already afraid it might be too much without real lube. I'm not hung like Daveman, but damn she's tight. A rookie."

"Bathroom cabinet, over the sink." She gasped when Dave and Neil moved in tandem in response to her admission.

James lurched to his feet before she could explain. It didn't matter to the crew. They wouldn't blink twice at her previous experiences.

"Kay, you still have a good two inches left on Dave, can you take more?

Do you want to?" Neil's fingers flittered across the taut tissue between her ass and pussy.

Dave's groan preceded a jerk of his hips that embedded him deeper in her swollen pussy. She shrieked. The invasion had lights dancing behind her scrunched eyelids.

"Sorry, baby." Dave apologized through gritted teeth. "Keep your hands off my balls, Neil. She feels great. Refuse to hurt her."

"I can take it." She gasped as she sat up. Gravity embedded more of his cock in her pussy. She slid down his tool until her clit tapped the pad of muscle above his shaft. Maybe she'd lied. His girth stole her breath.

"That's a good girl." Neil petted her ass until she stopped clenching.

The pressure eased, morphing from too much to just right. "Yes!"

Kayla rotated her hips in a tiny circle, desperate to build friction on the tight knot of her clit. The motion caused

Dave's blunt head to nudge ultra-sensitive nerve endings deep in her pussy. They both groaned when she strangled the base of his cock with the ring of muscles at her entrance.

Dave gave the silver hoops in her nipples a few playful flicks with the calloused tip of his finger before cupping her shoulders and bringing her close to his chest once more. The pounding of his heart ricocheted through her right breast.

"You're so beautiful, so right, I wonder if I'm still dreaming," Dave whispered against her lips between soft, sweet kisses. "I had the most amazing dream of you last night. Do you want to hear it?"

"Yes." She stared into his eyes, deeper, darker now that arousal swamped him.

"Later, kids." James skid next to them like a baseball player stealing home in a world-championship game. "Look what I found."

He rattled the cardboard box containing the tube of unused lubricating jelly she'd gotten for free with one of the toy orders she'd placed online. She hadn't needed it with her neon-pink vibrator.

"Good work." Neil consumed his lover's mouth as he transferred his bounty. "Maybe if you're nice, I'll find some other uses for this later."

"Mmm." James shivered beside her.

Kayla broke from Dave's mouth with one last, lingering kiss. She grinned when he winked and nodded. They reached out together. Her hand landed high on James's thigh. Between the pressure she added to the svelte muscles there and Dave's grip on James's waist, they positioned him where they preferred.

She bent toward her prize, engulfing his proud cock in one bold swoop. His balls dragged across Dave's parted lips. A small spurt of precome landed on her tongue when Dave opened wide to lave the bunched skin of James's tight sac with the flat of his tongue. He must have done a good job. More salty fluid oozed from James's cock.

Kayla savored the treat as pleasure eradicated what little inhibition she possessed.

"That's it," Neil coached her as autopilot took control of her body. She ground herself on Dave's cock, fucking him with tiny strokes that focused the ridges of his cock precisely where they did the most good. The walls of her pussy gripped his thick shaft.

"Are you going to come, baby?" Dave tilted his face to alert the men surrounding her to the early warning signs. "Come on my cock. Come on Neil's fingers. Come with James in your mouth."

Pressure built in her tummy. It rose like mercury in a thermometer on the hottest day of the year until she couldn't restrain the sensations overcoming her reason. She should wait—enjoy the anticipation. Wallow in rapture.

When Dave rolled his hips, increasing contact with her clit and Neil slipped a third finger in her ass, they defeated her. She screamed around James's erection, sucking him hard and fast in time to the contractions rippling her pussy around Dave.

Three strong partners held her up, grounded her, kept her from flying into space as her climax threatened to rip her apart. Pleasure smashed into her with reverberations that didn't seem to end. It slowed but kept pulsing in her core as Dave settled into a steady rhythm of thrusts from below that Neil matched in counterpoint.

"Hold on to it, Kay." James wove his fingers through her hair, positioning her where he pleased as he fucked her mouth. "Focus on the feeling. Grow it, keep it, tend it until it blossoms inside you again and again. You can do it. Ride the euphoria. Over and over. I've seen Morgan and Kate do it. Makes me wish I were a woman."

She didn't have a choice as their decadent stamina kept them hard and intent on satisfying her. They filled her with more desire than she could have imagined possible as recently as yesterday.

A particularly hard stroke from Dave sent her careening into another blast of bliss.

"Yes, yes," James chanted as he fed her his cock. "Just like that. Again, Kay."

The wet sounds of Dave tending to James's sac rushed to her brain, setting her off. A flood of come dripped from her soaked opening, saturating Dave's balls.

"There you go." Neil's fingers were forced from her ass by the rejuvenated convulsion of every fiber of her being. When he replaced them, they felt larger.

She whimpered around James's cock, inspiring a shudder from the man in her mouth.

"Keep going, Kayla." James rubbed her back, soothing even as he enflamed. Between the guys, six hands caressed her all over, driving her insane. "You'll come again when he penetrates you. Fills you."

She almost felt guilty for stealing James's fun. His reverent murmurs kept her from fearing the bite of pain she'd always experienced in the past. None of the crew would hurt her.

"You're ready." James moaned when the head of Neil's cock began to sink into her tense hole. "Push out now, keep breathing. Long and slow, sweetheart."

Kayla surrendered to their guidance. She let herself experience as her mind obeyed their commands without processing them. A swell of rapture carried her away when the mushroom head of Neil's cock breached the last of her resistance. He plunged inside, her ass swallowing him whole.

She shuddered in between Dave and Neil, packed, coming apart over and over just as James had promised. Her orgasms lingered and merged into one seamless expression of pure euphoria.

"Ah, yes." James crooned. "Like that. Just like that."

He slipped from her slack jaw, his expanded cock slapping Dave's chin. When she struggled to reclaim him, she ended up rubbing her lips over his shaft. The motion created a sandwich out of her and Dave's mouths, which slathered sloppy kisses on James's erection while he thrust between their eager lips and tongues.

Kayla stared into Dave's eyes as they delivered pleasure to his friend. She thought she read more than lust in the depths of his gaze but her ecstasy-hazed brain could have imagined it.

Neil pillaged her rear, invading deeper with every fluid glide while

James fucked their faces, the tip of his cock poking into either her or Dave's mouth on occasion. When it did, they sucked hard, drawing grunts from the slighter man at their side.

Dave's eyes rolled when Neil picked up the pace of his shuttling cock. The motion caressed Dave through the thin membrane inside her, eliciting a series of curses, pleas and groans from them all. She couldn't survive much more of this perpetual bliss.

The three men jammed her full—pussy, ass, mouth, heart and soul. Their genuine caring and commitment to gifting each other, including her, with as much pleasure as possible caused yet another burst of desire to obliterate her reasoning.

She rocked backward, enhancing each of Dave's and Neil's thrusts while increasing the frequency of the flickers of her tongue, which brushed along the head of James's cock. Dave's hard-on swelled impossibly inside her. Neil choked her hips in a bruising grip.

They pounded inside her, racing for the finish line.

James watched them all through slitted eyes, his long eyelashes dragging on his flushed cheeks. "Now."

His shout shattered the spell like a sonic boom. He threw back his head and groaned.

"Fuck, yes." Neil's abdomen slapped her ass a few more times then froze, impaling himself deep within her. "Now."

Dave roared a moment before molten liquid flooded her pussy. He consumed the strands of semen erupting from James's cock as he gifted her with jet after jet of his own pearly come. Neil surrendered, depositing his release into her ass. The proof of their satisfaction singed her, triggering one last tsunami of passion.

She writhed between Dave and James, crying out her appreciation. Neil withdrew his softening cock from her body and collapsed on the floor behind his mate. She didn't realize she mewled, her body shuddering with the remnants of passion, until all three men began to soothe her. Dave rolled to his side, facing his friends, cradling her close to his bellowing chest.

"You're fine, Kay. Don't panic." He panted into her hair with rough breaths. "Overwhelmed, that's all. Let it fade. Relax. Float down slow. We have all day. You were amazing. Did great."

She tried to settle, but the lingering twinges of her ass and pussy sent sparks up her spine, jolting her back to the intensity of their encounter, time after time. James slithered down her torso, petting her, calming her. He tapped her hip, pressing until she rolled to her back.

The twisting motion dislodged Dave's cock—impressive even half-hard.

Come dribbled from her enlarged pussy, running into the seam of her cheeks. The rivulet of fluid triggered another arc of electricity to ping her over-sensitized clit.

"No more." She moaned and scrunched her eyes closed.

Dave cupped her cheek and placed tender kisses at the corner of her mouth until she turned, accepting his gentle distraction. He held her immobile when James descended, cleaning her, pacifying her with tender laps of the flat of his tongue.

Kayla squealed and tried to evade the initial intensity. Neil and Dave rubbed her arms, her chest and her belly until the overstimulation melted into something delicious.

She sighed as she went boneless in their grips.

James sipped the last of their fluids from her pussy and ran his tongue over the glazed portal of her ass, until all scraps of tension abandoned her body.

He laid his cheek on her belly and surrendered, as though savoring his own colossal relief.

She might be sore for a week, but it had been worth it.

CHAPTER SIX

Kayla snatched her apron from the magnetic hook on her refrigerator and tied the string in the back before preparing her grandmother's famous chicken soup along with extra salty-caramel hot chocolate for dinner. The guys would probably appreciate the heat.

She glanced out the window over the sink and giggled as they chased each other around the driveway, which they'd spent the last few hours clearing, embroiled in a massive snowball fight. Damn, they looked more scrumptious than the meal she assembled as they ran, dodged, tackled and shouted. Their open coats and soaked jeans would chill quickly in the setting sun.

The storm had passed sometime during the night. A little more than two feet of fluffy white precipitation had added up. After a few hours lounging around, telling stories of the years they'd known each other and asking about her history, the three men had paced the cabin, stir crazy.

Accustomed to physical exertion, they didn't do well idle.

She'd hinted at a million naughty ways to pass the time. If they noticed her innuendo, they'd done a brilliant job of hiding it. By mid-afternoon they'd decided to shovel the deck and porch to relieve the weight from the structure. They hadn't stopped until tidy paths led from the house to the generator and to the wood shed. The entire driveway had been cleared too.

The soup pot began to bubble, demanding her attention.

Not long after she'd dropped in chunks of onion and carrots, the back door opened and a racket the likes of which her little house had never known pre-crew echoed through her laundry room. Boots clattered to the hardwood floor. Curses followed when clumps of snow landed on bare skin.

"Leave everything in there and I'll wash it," she shouted over the ruckus of three men in a tiny room.

"Thanks, Kay." Neil grinned as he emerged first, chaffing his arms. "I'm gonna grab a shower. Fucking freezing."

"If you're cold, please put some clothes on. You don't have to be naked all the time because I'm a naturist." She peeked over her shoulder at James and Dave, who followed shortly after their friend.

"Just don't check out my package for a few minutes, all right?" Dave cupped his palm over his crotch. He grinned as he strode to her bar and kicked out a stool.

James disappeared with Neil. The patter of the shower kicked on a few seconds later.

"Aprons don't count as clothes?" Dave gave a low whistle when she spun toward her meal in progress. White canvas framed her ass, putting it on display for the man lounging at the counter.

"Safety first." She winked at him as she passed by, intending to retrieve a lid from the storage space beneath the bar.

He snagged her around the waist and drew her to his side. His broad hands surrounded her cheeks, his fingers massaging the back of her head as he kissed her with a double dose of sugar and a hint of spice.

"What was that for?" She sighed, her heart skipping a beat.

"Your apron says, 'Kiss the cook!'"

She glanced down at her chest and laughed. "I guess it does, doesn't it?"

Was it too much to hope the easy familiarity they'd enhanced over the past day would last? The guys hadn't touched her since their wake-up fun—which had led straight to a mid-morning nap—at least not with intent to set her non-existent panties on fire.

Were they showing her there was more to their friendship than sex, or had they already gotten all they wanted?

"Dinner should be ready in fifteen minutes or less. I'll get the laundry going as soon as I set this to simmer."

"You don't have to wait on us, baby." He smiled. "Though, I'll admit it's kind of nice."

"I don't mind." She didn't lie. Making a home for the men felt right. Someday, she hoped for a family of her own to pamper. Until then, she'd have the guests at the spa. Making people comfortable was a gift of hers.

"Probably not a bad idea either." Dave rubbed the back of his neck. "Mike called about an hour ago. Looks like they're making decent progress on clearing the roads. He thinks they'll be able to break through sometime tomorrow. Maybe before breakfast."

"Wow. That's…fast." She hadn't expected their time to end so soon.

"I know."

"Who died in here?" James traipsed into the kitchen, scrubbing his hair with a towel. Neil snapped him on the ass with his own wet terrycloth. The two men engaged in a mock-battle, oblivious to the questions zinging around the room.

"Hurry up, Dave." Neil shoved his friend toward the bathroom. "I'm starving. Don't want to wait once dinner's ready."

Kayla slid a sheet of rolls into the oven, wringing a groan from one of the men when she bent to adjust the racks. By the time she straightened, Dave was nowhere in sight.

Did it bother him to leave not knowing where they stood? She wished she could talk to him alone. Maybe tonight they could whisper in the shadows when Neil and James slept. It might be fun to plot their course like two clandestine lovers.

She grinned as she stripped off her apron and headed for the laundry room, passing the bathroom on the way. Dave's off-key rendition of Bruno Mar's section of "Nothin' On You" cracked her up and gave her hope as she shoveled their soggy sweatshirts and sexy jeans into her washing machine.

When only a pile of their socks and boxer briefs occupied the corners of her laundry basket, she tipped it into the circular opening, wondering at the heft remaining in the plastic tote. A resounding clunk startled her into releasing a ridiculous squeak.

"You okay?" Dave must have heard it too.

"Yeah."

"What was that?" he shouted from the room next door as he closed the taps. A moment later he poked his head around the corner.

She rummaged in the machine for source of the racket. "No idea."

"Why don't I finish this up for you?" Neil burst into the space as her fingers landed on something cool and heavy in the sea of fabric. Make that a couple of somethings.

"What the hell?" She rescued the objects from the washer, holding them up so the guys—including Dave—could see. "Someone missing a pair of...doodads? What are these things anyway?"

"Oh shit." Neil's eyes bulged. James crashed into Neil's back when his lover stopped short. He knocked Neil the rest of the way into the room.

"Tell me I'm not seeing this." Dave turned an unhealthy shade of purple.

"Somebody better start talking." Kayla's throat burned with acid. The guys shifted from foot to foot without fulfilling her command. She dropped the basket and set the objects on top of her dryer very carefully before saying again, much softer this time, "What are those?"

Neil cleared his throat. "They're spark plugs."

"What—" *Spark plugs. Oh, no. Spark plugs.* "As in a pretty fucking integral part of a truck engine?"

"Son of a bitch." Dave propped one hand on the frame of the bathroom doorway and lowered his head. "I *knew* it didn't sound right. You little shit."

"You tricked me?" She tried not to panic, but her breathing grew erratic and her stomach plummeted to her toes. "Why?"

No one said a word.

"You planned *this*?" She couldn't seem to make her brain understand what her heart already grasped. They'd cooked up a scheme to corner her alone. To worm into her bed…or onto her floor, as it happened. Her laugh sounded twisted even to her own ears. "Joke's on you then. All you had to do was ask to fuck me. I wanted you bad enough I would have bent over for you before the storm and you could have been on your merry way, without having to sacrifice the whole weekend."

"Jesus," Neil snarled. "That's not what—"

"Shut up, asshole." Dave silenced Neil with a slice of his hand through the air. "You've done enough, don't you think?"

"Four pissed off people in a tiny cabin. Awkward. You should have considered that before you lied to get your jollies." She stormed past the three men staring at her.

Dave didn't try to stop her from running or attempt a lame excuse. He let her go. Maybe it was easier for them both to end things quick.

Painless.

Except it hurt like hell.

"I'll stay upstairs until you can leave in the morning. Let yourselves out."

***

Kayla broke her promise not to look out the window. Minutes after the buzz of small engines shattered the ultimate stillness of the mountain, and her cabin, she stole a glance out of her bedroom. The crew, all of them, hadn't left. Three snowmobiles littered her frosted yard. Neil, James and Dave stood in a half circle, their hands jammed in their coat pockets. They faced Mike and Joe— along with two women who could only be Kate and Morgan.

From inside, Kayla couldn't hear their conversation. Their faces spoke volumes. The men headed for the transportation. A sob cracked her resolve not to shed another tear over the studs who'd rocked her world then shattered her dreams.

The women stood their ground. When Mike waved, encouraging them to hop on the snowmobiles, the shorter one shook her head. Instead, she grabbed the other woman's hand and marched toward the cabin.

Maybe she needs to use the bathroom. Please, please, just have to pee.

No such luck.

"Hello?" A friendly greeting filled Kayla's sanctuary along with the whisper of snow jackets shedding onto her foyer floor. "Sorry to intrude, we know you're here and probably don't want to talk to us—"

"So what are we doing, Kate?" The other woman spoke softly, but her question carried. Unlike the hushed argument Dave, Neil and James had had the night before. Kayla's hitching sobs had obscured the sound carrying across the short distance in that case.

"We're coming up, Kayla."

"I'm naked." She hoped to scare them off.

"Nothing we haven't seen before," Morgan chimed in, supporting her friend's decision. Kayla hated the jealous pout overtaking her face for a moment.

The two women reached the top of the stairs and took in the tight quarters. "This place is super cute. I'm Kate."

"Hi." Kayla smiled despite herself at the woman's direct approach and her refusal to avoid looking at Kayla's nudity.

"Morgan." The other woman held out her hand, but didn't stop with a shake. She leaned in and hugged Kayla. "I'm sorry we had to meet like this. I've heard bunches about you."

"Are you okay?" Kate sat cross-legged on the end of her bed. "Dumb question, I know. It wasn't right to leave without coming to see how you're doing first. Can we do anything for you?"

"How about finding me a new construction crew so I don't have to be mortified every day when your guys come to work?" Kayla crashed into the pile of pillows on her bed then buried her face in her hands.

"If anything, Neil, Dave and James are the ones who should be ashamed." Morgan patted her knee.

"It was Neil who thought up this brilliant scheme." Kate rolled her eyes. "It's hard to believe now, but he meant well. He played matchmaker. Not like you four needed any help."

"Yeah, Dave didn't know anything about it," Morgan chimed in. "He's kicking himself because he heard the difference in the engine and still didn't force the issue. I think he was glad for the chance to stay. He's been dying to ask you out for weeks."

"It's true. It broke his heart to hear you crying up here last night, assuming you wouldn't welcome his comfort." Morgan put a hand on Kayla's shoulder. Though they'd just met, Kayla went with it, resting her head on Kate's thigh. "I know it doesn't fix what they did, but they're guys. Pretty awesome most of the time—"

"And dumb as shit the rest." Morgan rolled her eyes.

The door opened and shut once more. No one spoke up. Kayla swore she could smell Dave's unique scent, a combination of oak and cinnamon.

"Will you hear him out at least?" Kate vouched for one of her fiancé's best friends. "I'm sure he won't screw up again.

"I can't promise that." Dave's baritone lacked its usual luster. He climbed the stairs slowly, giving her the chance to throw him out. She didn't. "But I'll try my best to make you happy."

His nostrils flared when he spotted the three women sitting together.

The gaze scanning her form made her feel vulnerable in the nude for the first time in her life. Another thing he'd promised to understand then ruined.

"We'll wait outside." Kate and Morgan inched toward the stairs. "No matter what, we'd like to hear from you. Maybe we can have lunch sometime soon?"

"I'd like that." Kayla realized her polite response held more than a kernel of truth. "Thank you."

Dave waited until they shut the door behind them. "Kay, I'm so sorry."

"For what?" If he really had been in the dark about Neil's plotting, why hadn't he said so?

"For ignoring the facts. For letting myself go along with something I knew was wrong even if I didn't figure out all the details. For backing down without a fight. For leaving you to suffer last night. For hurting you." He deflated, sinking to the edge of her mattress.

"Kate and Morgan informed me I fucked up at every turn."

Kayla couldn't help it. She laughed through the tears stinging her eyes.

"Truly, I'm so very sorry." He reached out and touched her hand. "If nothing else, for ruining the brief time we did have together. I'll never forget that."

Instant sparks arced from the point of contact throughout her body. "I forgive you. And Neil. Thanks for coming in to straighten things out. At least now I won't feel so awkward when you come to work."

He stared at her so long she thought she might have misunderstood.

"Unless you don't plan to finish the job. If you give me recommendations—"

"We *always* finish the job." Dave leaned closer, treating her to the spice of his skin blended with her shower gel. "Don't you want anything more me, Kay? Or did I ruin what I thought we had?"

"Me? You're the one who backed away. Even before the...incident. You didn't touch me at all after yesterday morning."

"I saw you wince when I pulled out." He closed his eyes and breathed deep for a minute. "You were tender. We didn't want to hurt you."

"I thought..."

"Oh, crap." He stared at her with dilated pupils. "You thought what? That I'd taken my fill? That I'd gotten what I came for?"

She bit her lip and nodded.

Dave shot to his feet and opened the window. He shouted out to his friends. "Go ahead without me. I'm staying."

A round of cheers, hoots and claps had a blush rising to her cheeks.

"Tell Kay I'm sorry." Neil's shout rose above the crew's celebration.

"See you tomorrow," Joe called up a moment before engines, with fully functional spark plugs, hummed once more.

"Baby." Dave took a deep breath as he climbed into her bed and lay down beside her. "I haven't given you a reason to trust me yet. I'll prove myself to you however it takes. Yeah, you're sexy as sin and I love watching you come apart. I admire your adventurous side in and out of bed and hope to indulge it. Regularly. More than that, I adore your spirit, your laughter and your all-around brightness. I'd love to have you as part of my life. For the long run. Above all, I'm praying right now that your soul is as attracted to mine as mine is to yours. That you want to join my family, the crew, and make me the happiest guy in a two state radius. The king of this mountain."

"Only if I can be your queen."

"I never considered you a plaything." He nibbled her knuckles as if paying homage. "I'll kick Neil's scrawny ass for making you doubt my commitment for even an instant."

"Can we take things slow?" She admitted part of her reluctance stemmed from her own actions. She'd rushed into bed with him. The rash decision had eroded her confidence in their compatibility outside of the most magnificent sex of her life. The intensity of the chemistry they generated shocked her. Frightened her. Would it last? She hoped it could.

"Of course." He opened his arms. "Whatever it takes."

Kayla slid into his embrace and felt like she'd come home. She smiled against Dave's cotton-covered chest. "I'm so glad you came back."

"I'll never leave you again." He stroked her hair from her cheek, lulling her toward a nap after their restless night. "You're stuck with me."

She burrowed deeper into him, resting her hand above the steady beat of his heart.

"Sleep baby, I've got you. Maybe you'll have a dream as great as the one I had two nights ago."

"You never told me about it," she mumbled.

"It was crazy. Vivid. The most realistic one I've ever had. I saw you and I together, at Mike and Kate's wedding. You were gorgeous in a light green dress."

"I hate dresses."

He chuckled. "You'd wear one if it made Kate happy."

She couldn't argue.

He took a deep breath then whispered, "A diamond ring sparkled on your finger as we danced and twirled under the lights on the spring evening. I could smell the flowers. It was magical. Perfect. Only odd thing was you kept looking over your shoulder to a table where Neil and James sat."

"They wouldn't miss Mike's wedding for the world." She couldn't address the rest of his vision—her chest ached at the image and she swore she could picture it too. Crazy.

"No, but they weren't alone."

"What?" She tried to focus. Instead, she slipped away. The last of her anxiety fled, stealing her starch.

"Weird." He mumbled as he cradled her closer. "A woman sat between them, and she kept smiling at you. At us. Anyway, it was nice."

"Sounds like it."

He kissed her temple then whispered, "Sweet dreams."

They were sweet.

And *extra* naughty.

Through every one, Dave stayed by her side.

WHAT HAPPENS TO NEIL, JAMES,
AND THE REST OF THE CREW?
KEEP READING TO FIND OUT!

DEVON'S PAIR
POWERTOOLS
JAYNE RYLON
NEW YORK TIMES BESTSELLING AUTHOR

Will his boyfriend's girlfriend become his girlfriend too?

James has watched each of the crew fall in love, one by one, until only he and his life partner Neil remain "unattached". So, when he sees the way his bisexual boyfriend is checking out their new apprentice, he's sure he's doomed to lose the man of his dreams.

His love is strong enough that he would let go to ensure Neil's happiness. Instead, sparks fly between the three of them—along with the rest of the crew—and he realizes he might not have to surrender because his boyfriend's girlfriend is becoming his girlfriend too.

Warning: The world's first m/f/m/f/m/f/m/m/f...we think. You never know exactly what's going to happen next when the crew gets back together, but it's guaranteed to be steamy.

EXCERPT FROM DEVON'S PAIR, POWERTOOLS BOOK 4

Neil swiped work-scuffed knuckles over his gaping lips to ensure no drool escaped. He couldn't help but stare. Painted toes peeped from strappy sandals. They led his bulging eyes to a delicate ankle then up the pretty, tanned calf that poked beneath the open door of a beastly black truck. The sexy shoe rested on the running board before its equally delicious owner hopped down to street-level right outside the crew's current fixer-upper.

Maybe the pick-up wasn't any bigger than the one he and James owned. It could have been the sultry yet petite driver who made it seem as enormous as the whale sharks he and his boyfriend had spotted while snorkeling in Mexico last year. There too, most anything would have seemed gargantuan beside the glorious plum smuggler that had hugged James's svelte hips as though he'd been shrink-wrapped into it.

Neil shook his head to clear the tropical memories of his lover. Between them and the chance run-in with this woman—one he'd love to lure inside and share with James—he'd be sure to sport wood when he met their new employee.

The lecture James had delivered on their ride in this morning resounded in his mind. "Try to tone it down until we get to know him, okay? The new guy might not be as accepting as the rest of the crew of our wild liaisons."

Not many people were.

Wouldn't be good if their recently hired apprentice quit before lunch.

The dude hadn't showed yet, which meant Neil had to hang out here on the curb and wait for the schmuck. A mutual friend had highly recommended

Devon Giles right when they'd decided they could use some temporary help. Most of the rest of the crew settled into new relationships and needed a little extra personal time compared to usual. After a bunch of debates, they'd agreed to try adding someone to their tight-knit group on a trial basis.

Running late on day one wouldn't earn the guy any brownie points.

Still, the sweet view made up for abandoning James, who'd already started tearing up the old flooring by himself. Neil hated to let his partner shoulder more than his fair share. Generous and hardworking, his mate would push himself harder than he should. Neil swore he'd make it up to James with a killer back rub and slow, relaxed sex.

Maybe sooner rather than later if he ate his fill of such sweet eye candy.

The woman sauntered around to the other side of her truck and caused Neil to wonder if he was dreaming when she shucked her cornflower blue peasant blouse right there in the soft light of the spring morning. She left her racer-backed sports bra in place as she kicked off those sinful shoes and covered her cute pink pedicure with thick white socks before slipping her dainty feet into sturdy...construction boots?

What the—?

ABOUT THE AUTHOR

Jayne Rylon is a *New York Times* and *USA Today* bestselling author. She received the 2011 RomanticTimes Reviewers' Choice Award for Best Indie Erotic Romance.

Her stories used to begin as daydreams in seemingly endless business meetings, but now she is a full-time author, who employs the skills she learned from her straight-laced corporate existence in the business of writing. She lives in Ohio with two cats and her husband, the infamous Mr. Rylon.

When she can escape her purple office, Jayne loves to travel the world, SCUBA dive, take pictures, avoid speeding tickets in her beloved Sky and—of course—read.

www.ingramcontent.com/pod-product-compliance
Lightning Source LLC
Chambersburg PA
CBHW060746210726
48292CB00015B/2793